My dad often tells me to watch out
because I'll make him blow a gasket.
But he always tells me too late,
after he's already blown it.

For my son, Janó

ÉVA JANIKOVSZKY

Just Who Does This Child Take After?

ILLUSTRATED BY LÁSZLÓ RÉBER

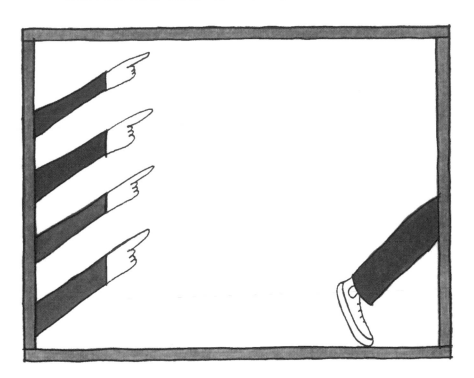

MÓRA PUBLISHING HOUSE

The translation was made
on the basis of the following edition:
Janikovszky Éva: Kire ütött ez a gyerek?
Móra Publishing House, Budapest, 2007

Translated by
ANDREW C. ROUSE

ÉVA JANIKOVSZKY LITERARY FOUNDATION
Your donations are greatly appreciated!
Tax Identification Number: 18114933-1-41
Bank Account Number: 10700024-45441406-51100005

www.janikovszky.hu

When I was little and clever, and kind and pretty everyone knew who I looked like.

Grandma said, "Goodness, he looks just like his mother!"

Granddad said, "The spitting image of his father!"

Uncle Emil said, "He sounds just like Aunt Iolanthe!"

My daddy said, "It's as though I was looking at myself!"

And mummy said, "Well, maybe he looks a little like me, too!"

When I was little and cleverer
than a grown-up,
my mummy wrote down

when I turned over from
my tummy
to my back,

when I
first
sat up,

 when I
stood up
in my pen,

 when I
first drank
from a beaker

and what my first word was.

When I was little and lovely,
everyone spoke to me like this:
Mummy's one and only joy
The light of Mummy's eyes
Darling angel
Little dear
Oh, I could just gobble him up
Let me kiss baby's iddy-piddy tootsies
What has mummy brought her darling baby?

When I was little and charming,
Daddy stuck photos of me in an album
so that everyone could see what I was like when I was

three days
old

two weeks
old

four months
old

one year
old

That's when my first
pair of outgrown baby-boots
ended up on the shelf
above Mummy's bed

and when
Grandma
cut off
a lock of my
lovely,
golden hair,

and when Daddy put my drawing in his purse.

When I was little, everyone was amazed at
how much I'd grown since last time,
what I'd said since last time
         and, well, how clever I was.

And Daddy took photos of me

         at the zoo,

                  in the playground,

                  with Caesar,
                  who I wasn't afraid of

                  and with Aunt Goldie,
                  who I was afraid of,

and at the end-of-year kindergarten celebrations,
where I was clapped the loudest.

Unfortunately you can't see in the photo
that I was interested in everything, that I was as lively
as a lizard and as sharp as a razor.

As long as I was little
and clever
and kind
and pretty,

whoever looked at me said,
"What a success story he is!"
"How proud of him you must be!"

And though the family
thought
that was
silly
and that
all little children are
as nice as each other,
still
among themselves
they did admit
that it was true
and that children
that were
at once so clever
and kind and
good-looking
were rare.

There, for instance, was
that poor Helen's boy

or poor Stephen's
daughter,

and then Grandma
remembered

was that Dennis

and everyone agreed
it would be better
not to speak
about Dennis.

Mummy and Daddy

smiled humbly at these times, and said
that of course they could all grow out of it.

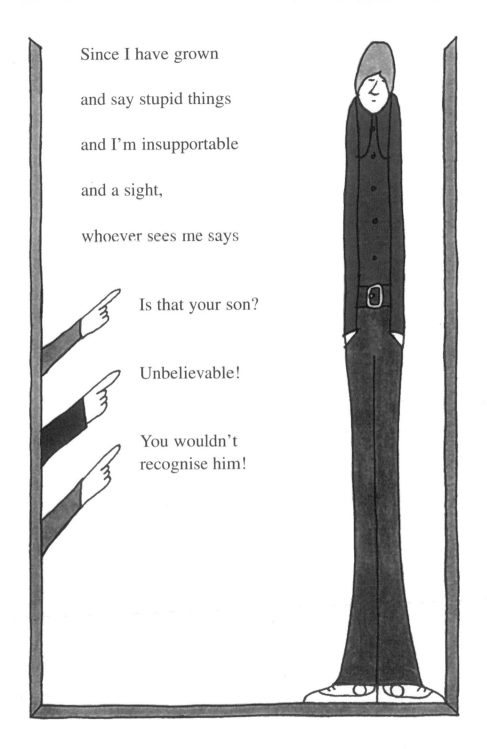

Since I have grown

and say stupid things

and I'm insupportable

and a sight,

whoever sees me says

Is that your son?

Unbelievable!

You wouldn't
recognise him!

And the family is ashamed, because of course
they weren't expecting me to grow out of it.

Now that I'm big
    and crazy and insolent and stupid,
        they just sit and sigh and wonder
            Who does this child take after?!

Grandma says
she doesn't know
who,
but it's definitely not
my mother.

Granddad says
he doesn't know
who,
but it's definitely not
my father.

Uncle Emil says
it's lucky
Aunt Iolanthe
didn't live
to see
this day.

Dad says,
"You shouldn't
let him
get away with
everything!"

and Mum says,
"'You're
his father.
Why don't you
hit him?"

And although the family knows very well
            that every adolescent is unbearable,
among themselves they still admit that too much is too much,
            that even their patience has its limits
            and that things can't keep going on like this.
It's just that they don't know exactly
            how they should be going on.

According to Grandma,
someone
ought to raise
this child properly,
because he's just
growing like a weed.

According to granddad
this child
should be taken in hand
more strictly,
because
responsibility
comes first.

According to Aunt Goldie
this child
should choose
his friends
more carefully,
because
once you mix
with the chaff
you eat
with the swine.

According to Mum
this child
should
sleep more,
because
he never
wakes up
fresh.

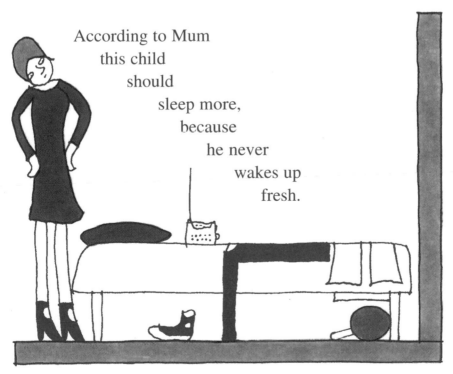

According to Dad
        this child
        should study harder,
        because
        like this
        he'll get
        nowhere.

According to Uncle Emil this is really sad
            as everyone was normal
                    in his family and he's afraid
                    that this is some of
                        Reginald's blood coming out.

I asked who
Reginald was,
but everyone
agreed that
Reginald
was
none of
my business.

I dreamt often of Reginald at that age,

but then grandma told me not to believe
my Uncle Emil,
and that Reginald
had been a good child,
it's just that
he had
dizzy spells,
and she
showed me
a photo as well.
Since then
I haven't
dreamt of Reginald.

Since I have been big and crazy and insolent and stupid
people haven't been able to speak to me. But they do.
Even though they know that if they speak to me
    it's like speaking to a brick wall.
I don't know why the wall doesn't answer,
but I don't because if I do there's only trouble.
Because, you see, I'm not even capable of answering.
If I'm asked Sweet Child
    what *do* you use your head for?
I answer that I use it for heading the ball,
    growing my hair,
    and my ears are stuck on it, too,
    and I can wiggle those.
Of course that's not good enough
for them,
because they
keep telling me
my head is
for thinking with.
If they ask me
what on earth
I was up to
all afternoon
that I'm only just doing
my homework
this late at night,

I could tell them that in the afternoon I recorded
three songs, then listened to them, then tried to write
down the lyrics, then looked for a dictionary
to help me, then found two postcards in the dictionary,
at which I was reminded of my postcard collection,
which had been in a large envelope, but of course
somebody had put it away, because they rummage
everything about, but even so I made a postcard
collection holder for my postcard collection,
because nothing can get lost in our family and
when I've found it then I'll put it in it, it really
was a good little postcard collection holder, it's just
that unfortunately the glue ran out over my desk
so I went hunting for some alcohol to dissolve it
and it did dissolve it but unfortunately the desk
varnish too so I looked for some varnish to varnish
it but there was something else in the rowboat
varnish box, because people are always just
chucking stuff anywhere, and I had to sand down
the whole thing, which reminded me
that it would be good to invent a kind of varnish
that you don't have to sand down but simply apply
and underneath there'd be another layer of varnish
that was still brand-new.
There might be another under that, but that's not
certain. Which reminded me that there were three
tasks to do for chemistry the next day, but I didn't
know which three, so I phoned Lazar because
he's brill at remembering that sort of thing, and he
really did know, and I played him the three new songs
I'd recorded over the telephone so he could hear
something normal, and that's when they came home.

Now if I said all that, then all
they'd understand is
that I'd ruined the desktop again.
So instead
I just
shrugged
my shoulders,
at which
they asked
who
I'd learnt
that
work tempo
from.
As though
I couldn't
find it out
for myself!
And anyway
in the end
they'll
just say
that they
don't know
what kind of
child I am.
And yet
they
all know
what kind of
child I am.
It's just me that doesn't.

According to
Grandma
the trouble is
that
this child
is nervous,

according to
Granddad
the trouble is
that
this child
doesn't do
any sports,

according to Aunt Goldie the trouble is that this child is introvert,

according to Uncle Emil the trouble is that this child's not interested in anything,

according to Mum the trouble is that this child is overburdened

and according to Dad the trouble is that this child doesn't think,

but they all agree
that I have no sense of decency.

I don't exactly know what a sense of decency is,
but my throat always goes dry
when the national side is on TV
and before the match,
they play the National Anthem

or whenever
we win
some contest
and up goes
the national flag,

and I still keep my old Teddy on my shelf

and I always feel bad
     if I catch a fish.

And it's not true either
that it never crosses my mind to help, because last time
I did the washing-up
at Ginnie's after the party and in the end I even washed
the kitchen floor.

Ginnie's grandma
even said

that Ginnie
should look upon me
as an example,

Of course Ginnie took revenge
and waited for Grandma outside the supermarket,
took her two
shopping-bags
and carried them
all the way
home.

Since then
I can also look upon
Ginnie as an example,
because she
may not be a beauty
but at least
she has
a sense of decency.

Of course they don't
understand
what I am doing
over at Ginnie's house
when there's
Stephen's daughter
living nearby,

or there's
Dennis's little sister,
who after all
is a serious little girl.

And why didn't I make friends with Dennis

when there was only good
to be learnt from little Dennis?

Because it's not normal either to be rotting away at home,
in the bad air, with the music forever blaring away.

At my age neither my Dad nor my Mum
    flopped about on the sofa in broad daylight,
    they didn't sit on the floor hunched over the tape recorder,
    but did their homework straight after lunch,

    and as soon as they'd done it
rushed outside to breathe the good air.

I reckon it's because neither Mum nor Dad had
                                        a tape recorder.

Whenever I play my tapes
Uncle Emil sighs and says
how much I loved music
when I was little

and Mum

thinks
that it's
not normal
I don't have
any
friends.

Because they don't believe I have any;
it's just that they also sit at home
hunched in the bad air,
with the tape blaring out all day.
They might even lie of the sofa in broad daylight.

Because of course
neither Mum nor Dad
have considered that
if I didn't have friends
there wouldn't be
anyone
who would lend me
the newest
recordings.

Dad says he's happy
that I have friends
but he'd like to see
who they are.
Then,
when they come
and he sees them,
then
he doesn't want
to see them.
What a rabble!
Not one of them
wiped their feet
when they came in,

and they all
had their hands
in their pockets,

and not
one of them
knew how to
greet you
properly,

but just
took
their shoes
off,

and not
one of them
used
normal words

because they
either neighed
like horses
or sat dumb
like
so many
oysters.

Because at my age my Mum and Dad didn't have
a tape recorder, or a record player, or a transistor radio,

but they did have good company
who they went out walking with, played parlour games with
and spoke with like intelligent beings.

All of Mum and Dad's friends
became great people

except
for those
who fell
by the wayside.

According to Grandma
you can't tell
which of my friends

is a boy
and which is a girl,
because they're all
dressed in the same gear
so it hurts
just to look at them.

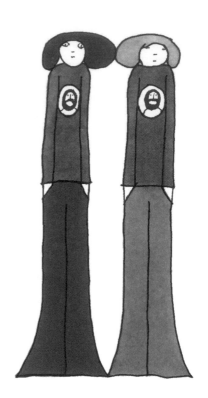

And if they don't all look the same
and you can tell
which are boys and which are girls
then it dumbfounds one

to see the liberties they allow
themselves:
well really,
do these girls have mothers
at all?

The funny thing is
that Ginnie's grandma
asked exactly
the same thing
the first time
I was over at their place,
even though she knew
I was a boy.

When everyone had seen my friends
here at home, my granddad said
that surely
I had enough
consideration
to see
my parents were
working people,
and they only had
one Sunday
and one Saturday before it
when they could rest a little,
so they'd like
at least then
some peace and quiet
in their own home.

I did have that much consideration and grabbed my tape recorder
     to take round to my friend's place.
Mum was happy that I was getting out and about
     and not sitting hunched in the bad air
or flopped out on the sofa in broad daylight,
          but she wanted to know my friend's name, address,
          last school results and father's job,
because she wasn't interested who was whose son
          because that didn't matter
but she was telling me there and then that I wasn't taking
that tape recorder anywhere because they hadn't spent
     all that money on it for other people to ruin it.
And that's because once Blaze took it
     and it just happened to go wrong then.
Then my dad had said,
          "I knew it, I knew it, I could have told you beforehand!"
Because grown-ups always know in advance:

that I'll
catch cold,

that I'll
ruin it

and also

that
things
will come
to a
sorry end.

I just
don't understand
why they're angry
when in the end
they're right.
I don't like
knowing anything
beforehand,
except the maths
problems
but I always ask
Lazar for them
anyway.

Since I've been big and my five-year-old little sister
has had more brains than me
everyone is curious as to
how my boy do you imagine your future?

As a rule
I should imagine my future
when my recorder is
turned up high,

when I
come
home
late,

when I leave
my muddy shoes
in the porch,
when I borrow
my dad's camera
for Blaze,

when
they can't
wake me up
in the
morning,

when I'm
a long time
in the
bathroom,

when I
watch TV
all day

and when
I spend all
my week's
pocket money
on Monday.

Of course
I can't imagine
my future then,
because
I'm occupied
with other
matters.

I do try to imagine my future
when I sit down to study,
because then I have the time,

or after a movie,
because then I'm in the mood,

or when Ginnie
whistles up to me,
because
that's when
it comes to mind.

I
think
the
future's
coming
along
fine
and
there's
no need to
muck about
with it,
I'm
doing OK
as the
future
comes
along
even if
it doesn't
show.

The reason I think it doesn't show
        is that otherwise they wouldn't be forever
                saying that other people would be happy

if they
could
live in
such a nice
home,

if they could
wear such an
expensive winter coat,

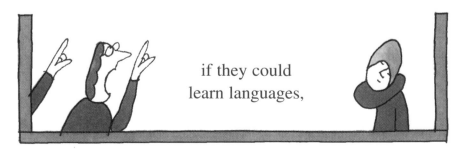

if they could
learn languages,

if they
could drink
cocoa
every
morning,

if they had so many books,
toys
and clothes,

and if their parents
spent so much time
on them.

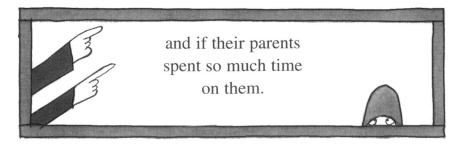

The only problem is that I don't even know what to do
when life is so easy.

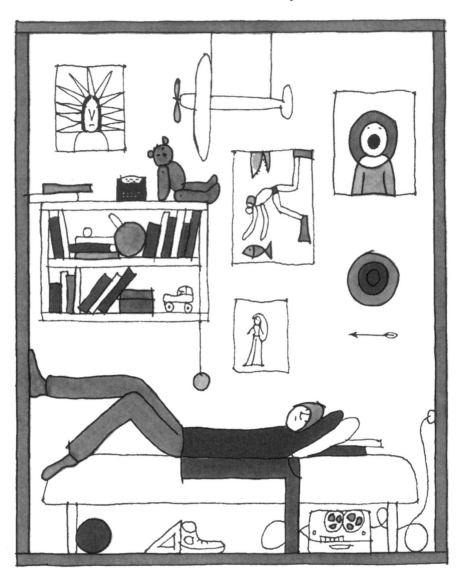

That's just not true,
    because I always know
        what to do
            when life
                is easy.

And I know that
      when I've grown up

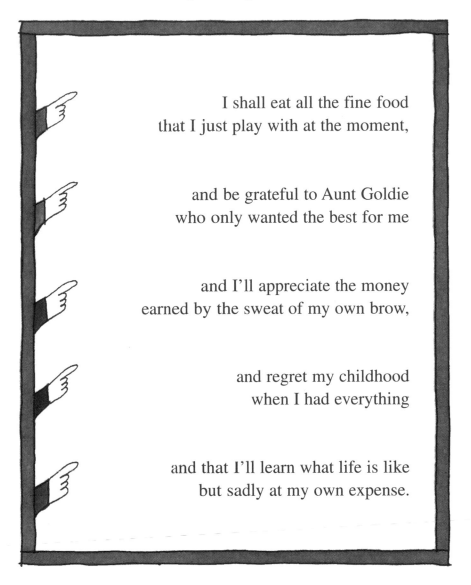

      I shall eat all the fine food
that I just play with at the moment,

      and be grateful to Aunt Goldie
who only wanted the best for me

      and I'll appreciate the money
earned by the sweat of my own brow,

      and regret my childhood
      when I had everything

      and that I'll learn what life is like
but sadly at my own expense.

The trouble is
      that none of these things is so important
        as to make me rush to grow up,
          and anyway
            I love leaving things to the last moment.

It's no good my dad
asking me
what kind of person
I'll become

because
I
haven't
the slightest
idea,
though
I've thought
about it
often
enough.

Maybe I'll grow another three inches,
but one for certain,

and
I'll
wear
shoes
a size
or two
larger,

and I hope my arm muscles will get
stronger
and my shoulders broader,

and I'll grow a beard.

But all the same
I'll look a little like Dad
and
I'll look a little like Mum

And when they're old, and they're sitting
on a bench in the park,
they'll show everyone
photos of me,
that this is their big boy,
you're sure to have seen him on television
and read about him in the papers
because he's world famous,
yes, he is,
and he's been there and done that and explored
and won and outstripped and broken records,
discovered and captured and saved,
overcome and freed and proclaimed,
lived through and written and set to music.

And then everyone will stand around them in a circle
and simply wonder and be amazed that
Goodness! Is that really your son?
Unbelievable!
You must be proud of him!
And at last not even my Dad will say,
"I knew it! I knew it!
I could have told you beforehand!"

ISBN 978 963 11 8610 9
Móra Publishing House, Budapest, 2009
Publisher: János Janikovszky
Printed in Hungary